W9-DFG-815

Congrats
on another
year of
You!

by
Marianne Richmond

Congrats on another year of You!

© 2004 by Marianne Richmond Studios, Inc.

All rights reserved. No part of this book may be
reproduced or transmitted in any form or by any means,
electronic or mechanical, including photocopying, recording
or any information storage and retrieval system,
without permission in writing from the publisher.

Marianne Richmond Studios, Inc.
420 N. 5th Street, Suite 840
Minneapolis, MN 55401
www.mariannerichmond.com

ISBN 0-9741465-7-9

Illustrations by Marianne Richmond

Book design by Sara Dare Biscan

Printed in China

Second Printing

TO JENN

FROM Liz

Date 2014

If someone
asked
you
today,

"how was your year?"...

What
would
you tell
them?

Would you say...
   "busy"

or "pretty good"

   or "not my best..."

or "fabulous"

   or something else???

Remember, as "cliched" as it sounds, life is lived in the everyday-ness. No matter how you'd sum up your year — you are to be congratulated, celebrated, cherished... for participating in and graduating from another year of life.

And doing it in a way
only you can do.

So...
think about it again.

"How was your year?"

Did you make someone smile
or laugh out loud?

Did you keep laughing...
    long after it was funny?

Did you share good conversation?

Gain a new insight?

Decide to do something?

Decide never to do <u>that</u> again?

Did you give a compliment that made someone's day?

Did you receive one

that made yours?

Did you
experience
the boost
of an
"I'm <u>so</u> glad
to see you"
hug?

How many times
did you say
the words,
"I love you"
or hear them
from someone
else?

Did you experience the strength (and sometimes complete frustration) of your emotions... from mad, sad, tired to happy, excited, silly?

All in one day? One hour?

Did you smell
the scent of a
spring morning... or
feel the chill
of a crisp night?

Did you get to feel the wind in your face while riding a bike?

Zipping along on in-line
skates? Walking?
Running? Pushing a
child on a swing?

Or just sitting
and being?

Did you help someone?

 Receive kindness? Feel special?

Feel proud of yourself?

Did you
exercise your
body and
give thanks
that all your
parts worked
pretty well?

Were you able to savor your
absolute favorite meal or dessert?

Did you experience the
delight of serving others?

Or the gift of being served?

Did you share
your abundance
with others?

Did someone
share theirs
with you?

Did you accomplish
something that
felt pretty daunting
at first...

and then celebrate
that you are
stronger than
you thought?

Congratulations
on living life
for another
365 days.

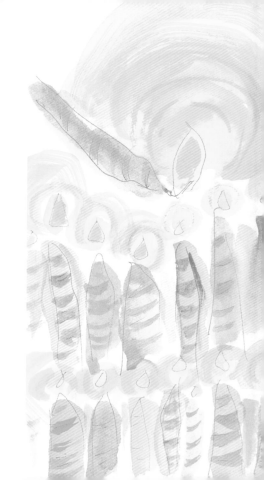

On discovering yourself,

paying your own way,

getting your car serviced,

your teeth cleaned,

your laundry done.

Congratulations on
being one year wiser.

On knowing
something new.

On having opinions
and sticking to them.

On enduring, surviving,
coasting, enjoying,
holding on and letting go.

Congrats
on
another
year
of
you!

A gifted author and artist, Marianne Richmond shares her creations with millions of people worldwide through her delightful books, cards, and giftware. In addition to the *Simply Said...* gift book series, she has written and illustrated four additional books: **The Gift of an Angel, The Gift of a Memory, Hooray for You!** and **The Gifts of Being Grand.**

To learn more about Marianne's products, please visit www.mariannerichmond.com.